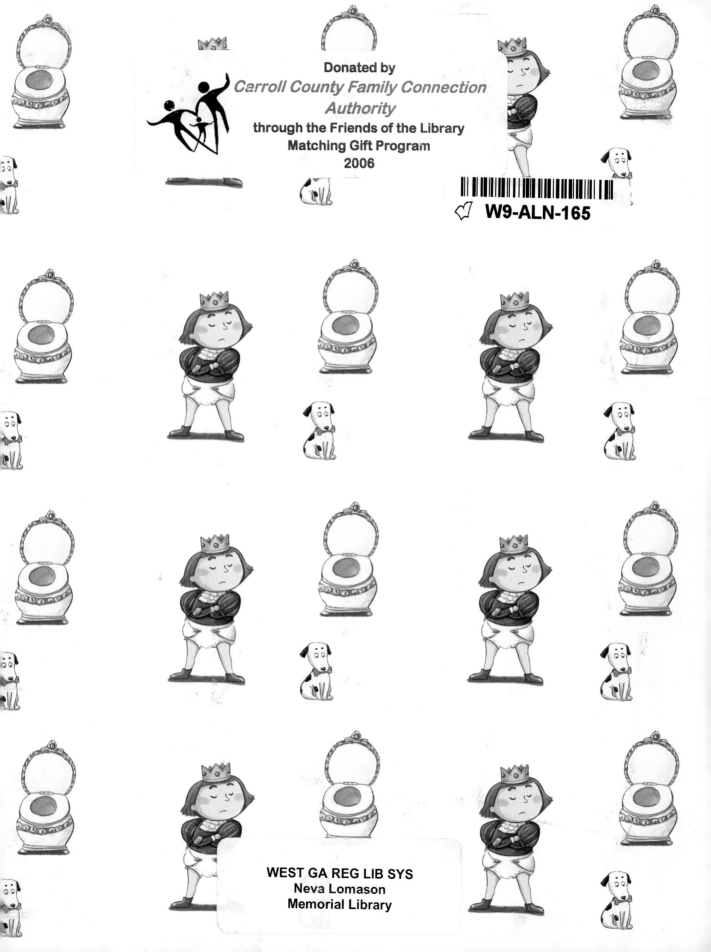

The PRINCE and the POTTY

Wendy Cheyette Lewison

Illustrated by Keiko Motoyama

Simon & Schuster Books for Young Readers

New York   London   Toronto   Sydney

$\mathcal{O}$nce upon a time there was a little prince who wouldn't use his potty.

"This potty is just your size!" said the queen.

"This potty is very handsome!" said the king.

But the prince said, "This potty doesn't please me!"
And that was that.

Now, the king and queen loved the prince just the same, of course. But the days passed by, and they worried that the prince would be wearing diapers forever and ever—even when he became king himself. And that would *never* do.

They decided to ask the Royal Wise Man for advice.
"Go get the prince a puppy," said the Royal Wise Man.

"A puppy? Why a puppy?" asked the king and queen. But
the Royal Wise Man closed his eyes and said no more.

So that very day they took the prince
to look for a puppy.

They traveled to the far reaches of the kingdom. They saw brown puppies and white puppies.

"Yip, yip!" said the puppy, wagging his tail.
"This puppy pleases me," said the prince.

So home to the castle they went. The puppy was given his own special bed to sleep in, right next to the prince's bed.

The puppy had his own special toys to play with . . .

. . . and his own special bowls to eat and drink from.
The puppy gobbled up his food and lapped up his water.

"Yip, yip!" said the puppy. Then he started to sniff around the floor.

Uh-oh.

"Oh, dear me!" cried the queen. "The puppy has made a puddle!"

"Bring me some cloth!" she called to the chambermaids.
"We must teach the puppy where to go," the queen said to
the prince.

"Here, Puppy!" she said.

"Here, Puppy!" said the prince. The puppy looked at the cloth. He wagged his tail.

"Yip, yip!" said the puppy. Then he grabbed the cloth with his little teeth and tore it up into tiny pieces!

"We must be patient," said the queen.

The queen sent for more cloth. And more. And more.
Day after day the puppy made puddles all over the castle.

Then one day the puppy made a puddle right in the middle
of the cloth—where a puppy *should* go.

"Hooray for the puppy!" said the queen.

"Hooray for the puppy!" said the prince.

The queen patted the puppy on the head and gave him a treat. She gave the prince a treat too—for helping. It was a big glass of peach punch.

Suddenly the prince had to go too.
Did he go in his diaper? No. Did he go on the cloth like the puppy did?

Of course not—that's silly! So where did he go?
He went where a prince *should* go.

There was a grand celebration at the castle. "Have you heard?" everyone whispered. "The prince has used his potty!"

"Hooray for the prince!" they cheered. "Hooray! Hooray!"

"Hooray for me!" said the prince, who was very pleased indeed. And what did the puppy say?

"Yip, yip!"

For my son, David Jon Lewison, the prince—W. C. L.

For Yuri and Miho—K.M.

SIMON & SCHUSTER BOOKS FOR YOUNG READERS
An imprint of Simon & Schuster Children's Publishing Division
1230 Avenue of the Americas, New York, New York 10020
Text copyright © 2006 by Wendy Cheyette Lewison
Illustrations copyright © 2006 by Keiko Motoyama
All rights reserved, including the right of reproduction in whole or in part in any form.
SIMON & SCHUSTER BOOKS FOR YOUNG READERS is a trademark of Simon & Schuster, Inc.
Book design by Daniel Roode
The text for this book is set in Golden Cockerel.
The illustrations for this book are rendered in acrylic on illustration board.
Manufactured in China
2 4 6 8 10 9 7 5 3 1
Library of Congress Cataloging-in-Publication Data
Lewison, Wendy Cheyette.
The prince and the potty / Wendy Cheyette Lewison ; illustrated by Keiko Motoyama.— 1st ed.
p. cm.
Summary: When the young prince refuses to use his potty, the king and queen are afraid he will wear
diapers all his life, until the Royal Wise Man suggests an unlikely solution.
ISBN-13: 978-0-689-87808-4
ISBN-10: 0-689-87808-7
[1. Toilet training—Fiction. 2. Princes—Fiction. 3. Dogs—Fiction. 4. Animals—Infancy—Fiction.]
I. Motoyama, Keiko, ill. II. Title.
PZ7.L5884Pqq 2005
[E]—dc22   2005019789